AND THEN COMES
Christmas

For
Santa

To Kaylan, my editor; Nancy, my wife;
June and Nancy, my sisters; and Ruth and Roy for my Christmases.
T. B.

For Harry and Hugo, and all of the Christmases we've spent together,
and all of the trees you have given names to. I love you.
J. C.

First edition 2014

Library of Congress Catalog Number 2013953455
ISBN 978-0-7636-5342-2

14 15 16 17 18 19 TLF 10 9 8 7 6 5 4 3 2 1

Printed in Dongguan, Guangdong, China

This book was typeset in Warnock.
The illustrations were created digitally.

Candlewick Press
99 Dover Street
Somerville, Massachusetts 02144

visit us at www.candlewick.com

AND THEN COMES
Christmas

TOM BRENNER
illustrated by JANA CHRISTY

CANDLEWICK PRESS

WHEN the days barely start and they're over again,
and red berries blaze against green shrubs,
and bare branches rake across the sky . . .

THEN hang boughs of fir or spruce or pine,
dotted with cones and bits of holly, welcoming winter.

WHEN frost glistens on pastures and fence posts,
and icy grass crunches underfoot,
and dark clouds sit low on the horizon . . .

THEN fill the windows with paper snowflakes
and frame the house with colored lights.

WHEN the red in the thermometer sinks toward the bulb,
and icicles cling to the edges of roofs,
and raindrops shift to feathery flakes . . .

THEN wrap yourself in layers and tumble out of doors to romp in snow as smooth as bedcovers.

WHEN elves and reindeer appear in stores,
and small trains race through toy villages,
and piles of presents nestle in cotton drifts . . .

Santa

THEN hop from foot to foot,
waiting to sit on Santa's knee.

WHEN cardboard boxes arrive and are quickly hidden,
and the neighborhood blinks with twinkly lights,
and empty lots turn into forests . . .

TREES
FOR
SALE

THEN head out and wander the rows
in search of the perfect tree.

WHEN Papa brings it into the house,
and Mama gets it to stand straight and tall,
and the room fills with that sweet piney scent . . .

THEN loop lights in graceful arcs,

place shiny balls just so,

and settle the angel on the very top.

WHEN winter break is just hours away,
and the programs and concerts are over,
and Mama's and Papa's gifts are done . . .

THEN sneak your treasures home,
and cut and wrap and tape with care,
and finish them off with ribbons and bows.

WHEN the days in December reach twenty-four,
and the sweet smell of baking fills the house,
and neighbors drop by with homemade goodies . . .

THEN hang your stockings where they can't be missed and tuck your presents beneath the tree.

Set out cookies and milk and plenty of carrots.

And with the sound of carols fading away,
snuggle in bed to hear those familiar words—
"'Twas the night before . . ."

WHEN one by one the lights go dark,
and the whispering and shushing dwindles off,
and the whole world seems to be waiting . . .

THEN, lo and behold, it's Christmas morning!

The milk and cookies and carrots are gone!

The stockings are stuffed fat!

And presents spill out from under the tree, begging to be opened!

AND WHEN Papa lights the fire,

and oohs and aahs and thank-yous sound around the room,

and wrapping paper covers the floor . . .

THEN gather at the table . . .

and bask in the magic of Christmas.